Don't Worry Throw Well

Matthew Dean

Published by Matthew Dean, 2025.

DON'T WORRY THROW WELL

First edition. June 11, 2025.

ISBN: 979-8231304783

Written by Matthew Dean.

Table of Contents

Dedication:

This book is dedicated to:

Ed "Sensai" Winstead,

You have been true pillar of the DWTW community. Your warmth, wisdom, and ever-present smile have left an indelible mark on all of us. Your spirit has brought joy, laughter, and a spirit of camaraderie we will never forget.

As you embark on the next chapter of your journey, know that you will be deeply missed. We send you off with our heartfelt wishes for health, happiness, and of course plenty of Bocce.

With love and affection,

Your

DWTW Family

Four Points to Glory

The early afternoon sun beat down on the polished clay courts of the Hill Country State Bocce Center, a sprawling, sun-washed complex nestled in the sleepy hill country town of Fredricksburg. Folding chairs creaked under the weight of longtime fans and first-time spectators alike. Coolers popped open. Shade tents flapped in the breeze. The air buzzed with excitement and the occasional clack of colliding bocce balls.

Four older men sat in a lopsided row of lawn chairs, each wearing a worn-out DWTW team t-shirt that had long since faded from black to soft charcoal gray. Depending on who you asked, the letters stood for Dell Webb The Woodlands, or Don't Worry, Throw Well.

Sensai sat straight-backed, legs crossed, a thermos of green tea in hand. With his crisp white beard and calm demeanor, he carried the quiet gravity of a man who could hit a leaf with a bocce ball from twenty feet. Beside him slouched The General, arms crossed, chin resting on his chest. His military haircut had grown into a disciplined silver mop. His eyes scanned the courts like a man watching enemy troop movements. The Destroyer, built like a retired linebacker with the smile of a mischievous teen, was halfway through a foot-long sub. And Mr. Annoying was living up to his name. With his sun visor pulled too low and his voice a constant buzz, he narrated every play as if auditioning for a sports broadcast no one had asked for.

"They're standing too close to the foul line again," he said, nudging The General. "That's gonna mess up their angles. Mark my words."

The General didn't respond. He rarely did.

They hadn't come to compete. The DWTW crew was here for the show. It was a chance to watch the state's finest teams compete in the annual playoffs. Drink some lemonade, and heckle a rival or two with good-natured jabs.

The first match of the day featured two top contenders: the Iron Balls and the Paesanos. Both teams wore matching uniforms and carried themselves with the swagger of minor-league pros. The opening tosses were fierce, clean, and methodical, until a disputed point turned into raised voices. One team accused the other of a foot fault. The other fired back with accusations of "ghost measurements." Within minutes, bocce balls were no longer the only things flying across the court.

Gasps rippled through the crowd as one of the Iron Balls shoved a Paesano. The Paesano retaliated by throwing a water bottle. A ref tried to intervene and got pushed aside for his trouble. Security jogged over with surprising speed.

When the dust settled, both teams were disqualified, leaving the tournament organizers scrambling. The announcer stepped up to the mic with a sheepish smile.

"Uh... folks, due to an... altercation... we're facing a slight delay. Both teams in Match One have been removed from the tournament. We're discussing next steps."

The DWTW team exchanged glances. Mr. Annoying was already halfway out of his chair.

"Well this is ridiculous," he muttered. "A whole day of bocce, ruined by hotheads."

The General stood. "It's not over yet."

Spectators grumbled. Someone nearby suggested refunds. One of the judges, a sharp-nosed woman in her sixties with a clipboard and an iron sense of order, was pacing near the court. Another was arguing with the remaining alternate team.

That's when Sensai stood.

He walked to the cluster of judges, his footsteps soft on the gravel. People around the court stopped to watch. The old man in the faded shirt looked like someone who had wandered in from a Tai Chi class. But when he spoke, there was a quiet confidence in his voice.

"If you need a team," he said, "we're here."

The judges blinked. One of them laughed. Another raised an eyebrow.

"You're not registered," said the clipboard judge.

"We're not here to win," Sensai replied, his tone as smooth as a river stone. "We're here to play."

A heated argument followed. There were rules, regulations, and reputations to uphold. With no viable replacements and a restless crowd growing louder by the minute, the judges faced an uncomfortable truth. Let these old guys play or cancel the most anticipated bocce event of the year.

After a long, reluctant pause, the head judge grabbed the mic again.

"Ladies and gentlemen... please welcome a last-minute substitution to the tournament: the DWTW team."

There was polite applause, mostly from friends and family in the crowd who knew them by name. A few boos slipped through, and one young hotshot was overheard saying, "This'll be over in fifteen minutes."

The DWTW team didn't care. They dusted off their old game shirts, adjusted their visors, and walked toward the court like a crew stepping onto a movie set twenty years after the credits rolled.

Sensai looked up at the sun. The Destroyer cracked his knuckles. Mr. Annoying started his commentary again.

"Well, here we go. Let's see if these old bones remember how to roll."

The General gave a rare smile. "Just don't fall asleep mid-throw."

As they took their positions, the crowd watched with curiosity, skepticism, and amusement.

DWTW's opening opponents, a sleek team of forty-somethings from Austin called The Precision Rollers, didn't smile once during warm-ups. They wore matching tracksuits and sported monogrammed bags with polished bocce balls.

Their captain had the grim efficiency of a surgeon and the cold focus of someone who hadn't smiled since 1999. In contrast, DWTW ambled onto the court like they were arriving at a church picnic. Mr. Annoying tripped over a rake someone had left near the sidelines. The Destroyer forgot what pocket he'd put his lucky coin in. The General squinted at the scoreboard like it was written in Morse code.

Sensai stood at the foul line, his first throw steady and elegant, nestling shy of the pallino. A respectable start. But it was all downhill from there.

The Precision Rollers moved like a machine. They knocked Sensai's ball away with surgical precision. Then they clustered three of their own around the pallino. DWTW tried to rally. The General's toss was a bit wide. The Destroyer overthrew by five feet. Mr. Annoying talked through his shot and managed to miss both the point and the silence.

By the seventh frame, it was 11–1.

The crowd looked, half embarrassed, half amused. Someone in the bleachers muttered, "Well, they gave it a shot." Another called out, "Hang in there, grandpas!"

When the match finally ended at 12–2, the DWTW team walked off to an awkward mix of applause and boos. They didn't talk much as they sat under the shade of their pop-up canopy. The General cracked open a Gatorade. The Destroyer muttered something about "sun glare." Mr. Annoying blamed the court's slope. Sensai sipped his tea and stared at the horizon.

Their second match was their last chance in the double-elimination format. They were scheduled to play a team from Dallas called Boccetoberfest. This team was loud, confident, and celebrating their "easy path" to the next round. They wore orange shirts with beer mugs on the back and high-fived between every point. They joked with the crowd, flexed after good throws, and didn't take the DWTW team seriously for a second.

That was a mistake.

Maybe it was the embarrassment of the first game. Maybe it was pride. Or maybe, just maybe, the magic of old friendships finally kicked in.

The General took over as strategist, calling shots like he was moving pieces across a battlefield. "Sensai, soft tap. Destroyer, power shot if they double-stack. I'll clean up."

The Destroyer, once wild and inconsistent, started hitting like a man who had trained in chaos. His throws bounced and skipped but somehow always landed in the right spot. He knocked enemy balls out with joyful grunts, raising his hands like a victorious gladiator.

To everyone's surprise, Mr. Annoying became a secret weapon. His nonstop commentary drove the Boccetoberfest team insane. He analyzed their every move, miscalled distances, offered unsolicited advice, and asked what time the next shuttle bus left as they lined up critical shots.

And Sensai... was Sensai. His focus never wavered. His throws were measured, graceful, and deadly accurate. He placed balls where they didn't belong and made them stay there with quiet dignity.

To the amazement of everyone, DWTW took an early lead and held it. The final frame came down to one throw. The Destroyer had a chance to seal the deal. The pallino was tucked behind a cluster of Boccetoberfest balls, but one clean hit could clear the way and give DWTW enough points to win.

The Destroyer grinned. "Time for some gentle destruction."

He hurled the ball with enough spin to curve inside the cluster. It clipped two enemy balls, knocked them aside, and rolled to a stop inches from the pallino.

Game over. DWTW 12, Boccetoberfest 11.

The crowd clapped, some even stood. No one had expected it. Least of all Boccetoberfest, who left the court muttering and shaking their heads.

With one win and one loss, DWTW had to play one more match to reach the finals. Their next opponents were The San Antonio Slicers. It was a gritty team known for cutthroat tactics and brutal accuracy. The Slicers didn't talk much. They let their throws speak for them.

The game was a war. Points went back and forth. No team ever held more than a two-point lead. The Slicers hit hard and precise. DWTW countered with creativity and teamwork. Sensai and The General developed a rhythm of setup and finish. The Destroyer went full berserker, slamming through obstacles with almost reckless joy. Mr. Annoying kept muttering, "You guys nervous yet?" loud enough for the other team to hear.

The pallino had landed near the back edge of the court. The Slicers had one ball positioned a few inches away. DWTW had none closer. One point and the Slicers would win.

Sensai stepped up with the last shot. The court fell quiet. He closed his eyes for a moment. Exhaled. Then, he released. The ball rolled with hypnotic

calm. Sensai's ball took its place.

The judge walked out with the measuring stick.

Then: "Point goes to DWTW."

Cheers erupted. The stands, once lukewarm on the DWTW team, were now on their side. People who hadn't cheered all day were on their feet, clapping, shouting, laughing. The underdogs had clawed their way to the finals.

As DWTW walked off the court, sweaty, sore, and stunned, The General allowed himself a small smile.

"Finals," he said, almost to himself. "How about that."

The Destroyer fist-pumped. Mr. Annoying started interviewing Sensai with an imaginary microphone.

Sensai looked up at the sky, then back at the court, and nodded.

The sun was beginning its slow descent behind the hills, casting a golden glow across the courts as the final match of the bocce tournament began. Spectators gathered in tighter, standing three rows deep behind the ropes. Phones were out, recording every moment.

It was the Cinderella team versus the reigning champions.

The DWTW team had gone from late-entry spectators to unexpected finalists. Now, they stood across from The Rolling Thunder. The team that had dominated the state circuit for five years. Everything about the champs was sleek and professional, from their form-fitting jerseys to the way their throws rolled down the court.

DWTW looked like they'd returned from a backyard cookout. Sensai stretched his shoulders. The Destroyer adjusted his headband, borrowed from someone in the crowd after losing his. The General scanned the court like he was counting enemy tanks.

And Mr. Annoying... looked rattled. For the first time since they arrived, he was quiet.

DWTW took an early 4–1 lead, stunning the crowd. The Destroyer landed a beautiful opening roll, nudging the pallino. The General followed with a soft-angled knock-off, pushing the champs' ball out and claiming another point. Mr. Annoying even hit one, an accidental but effective roll that everyone assumed was luck, and he did nothing to deny it.

But The Rolling Thunder didn't stay stunned for long. Frame by frame, the champs clawed back, point by point. Their throws became sharper, faster, and colder. They dissected DWTW's strategy with precision, exploiting every misstep. By the halfway mark, the scoreboard read 7–6 in favor of DWTW. Then it was 9–7, the champs in the lead. Then 11–7.

Mr. Annoying's throws had gone completely off. Wide, short, even one that bounced off the back wall. The General grumbled. The Destroyer gave him a fist tap anyway. Sensai said nothing, but when he walked past, he rested a hand on Mr. Annoying's shoulder.

Sensai's flawless placement and a defensive roll gave DWTW another point. The crowd leaned in. Whispers of "Can they really do this?" rustled through the air.

DWTW was down 11–8. The champs were locked in, smiling now, confident.

The pallino was thrown short. A dangerous spot. The champs opened with two perfect balls, one tight against the pallino, the other angled to block.

DWTW's first shots were desperate. The Destroyer knocked one wide. The General's throw rolled true but clipped the block and rolled an inch too far. Sensai managed to sneak one close, but it wasn't enough. With only one ball left to throw, DWTW was down by three and the champs were sitting with the winning point on the court.

All eyes turned to Mr. Annoying. He looked like he hadn't slept in a week. Sweat trickled from beneath his visor. He stepped up to the foul line, his bocce ball cradled like it weighed a thousand pounds.

"You got this," Sensai said.

Mr. Annoying looked back. "I've been off all game," he said, "I don't even know what I'm doing wrong."

"Maybe you're not doing anything wrong," Sensai replied, calm as ever. "Just throw."

The crowd was silent. The Rolling Thunder players folded their arms, waiting to celebrate.

Mr. Annoying exhaled. He bent down, took his stance, and let the ball go.

At first, it looked like another disaster. The angle was wrong. The pace was too quick. It headed directly for one of the champs' blocker balls.

A few people in the crowd gasped. Someone muttered, "No way."

The ball caught the side of the blocker and ricocheted, not out but inward, slicing the edge of the opponent's lead ball and knocking it sideways. It careened across the court and tapped the second ball knocking it away.

Mr. Annoying's ball now deflected, rolled into the cleared space… and stopped.

The judges approached with their measuring stick. Bending, squinting, lining it up.

Then the call came: "A Kisser. Four points—DWTW wins."

Cheers, whistles, and laughter filled the air. Hats flew. Someone in the back yelled, "Are you kidding me?!" A child shrieked, "THE OLD GUYS WON!"

The Destroyer lifted Mr. Annoying into the air like a sack of potatoes. The General cracked a smile so wide it might've broken his face. Sensai simply bowed his head, as if acknowledging something greater than himself.

Mr. Annoying, stunned, looked around in disbelief. "I did that?" he asked.

Sensai nodded. "You did that."

The Rolling Thunder players, to their credit, clapped. One even came over and shook Sensai's hand. "That was... incredible," he admitted. "You guys are something else."

As the DWTW team walked off the court, people reached out for high-fives, photos, and autographs. Someone handed The General a tiny trophy someone had made from a bocce ball glued to a soda can. He accepted it like it was gold.

A reporter asked Sensai how it felt to win. He paused, then replied, "We came to watch the game. But it sure feels good to win."

The team gathered under their pop-up tent, now surrounded by fans. Mr. Annoying flopped into his lawn chair, still shaking his head.

"We really won?" he said again, this time grinning like a kid.

"You really won," The Destroyer said, cracking open a cold soda. "And now, you're never gonna shut up about it."

Welcome Home

At Dell Webb The Woodlands, word spread faster than a golf cart in second gear.

The boys were back.

Folding chairs circled the bocce courts like satellites pulled into a joyful orbit. Cookie platters clinked onto plastic tables, and lemonade jugs emerged from coolers to a chorus of laughter and greetings. But today wasn't about watching bocce. It was about celebrating it.

At the far end of the court, a cardboard sign read:

WELCOME HOME DWTW

BOCCE KINGS OF FREDERICKSBURG

The DWTW team arrived to cheers and applause. Sensai led the way, calm and composed as always. The Destroyer trailed behind carrying a cooler over one shoulder and a bag of snacks in the other. Mr. Annoying waved like a politician, pointing at people he recognized. The General gave a curt nod, like a soldier returning to familiar ground.

"Look at 'em," someone muttered. "Back from the war."

"War?" another replied. "Please. It's bocce. And they won."

"That's what makes it a miracle."

The air buzzed with stories, each version slightly different, as people asked the same question in twenty different ways.

"You really beat the Rolling Thunder?"

"Wait, wait—Mr. Annoying hit the game-winner?"

"Did they seriously let y'all play without being registered?"

Mr. Annoying nodded. "Yup. Threw it on a curve, used the spin, kissed the pallino like I meant to do it." He mimed the shot. "Boom. Four points. Lights out."

The Destroyer snorted. "You tripped over your shoelace while throwing it."

"Details."

The General said nothing and sipped his Gatorade like he was still cooling down from battle. Sensai sat nearby, thermos of green tea in hand, his expression unreadable but peaceful. The chatter swirled around him like wind around a mountain.

A smaller group began to gather near the courts, where a few of the regulars started a casual game, the kind where no one kept score and the biggest conflict was whether the ball was closer or if they thought it was. Cookies made the rounds. Someone passed out little pins shaped like bocce balls. The Destroyer picked up a cookie shaped like a trophy, took a bite, and laughed so hard he nearly choked on it.

It felt good. Familiar. Like home.

As the sun dipped a little lower and the breeze kicked up through the Pines, Sensai stood.

He didn't raise his voice. He didn't need to.

Conversations stopped. Heads turned. Even Mr. Annoying, mid-sentence, paused.

"I have something to say," Sensai began. "And I want to say it with all of you here."

A beat passed. The quiet hung like dew.

"I'll be moving," he said.

A ripple moved through the crowd.

"Not for a few more weeks," he added. "But soon."

The Destroyer's face dropped. The General's brow furrowed deeper than usual. Mr. Annoying opened his mouth, then shut it again.

"You're serious?" someone asked.

Sensai nodded. "I've lived here a long time. Played more games on these courts than I can count. Lost a few. Won a few. Taught a few of you how to throw. Most of you ignored my advice," he added with a light smile.

Soft laughter broke the tension.

"But what matters," he continued, "is that this community, this game, it gave me something I never expected at my age. Purpose. Joy. And friends who yell at bocce balls like the balls can hear them."

That got a bigger laugh, even from The General.

"So yes, I'll be moving. But not far in the heart. I'll come back when I can. And until then, I expect someone to send me score updates. Preferably not Mr. Annoying."

"I'm your best option!" Mr. Annoying protested.

"And that," Sensai said, "is what I am worried about."

More laughter. More smiles. But the mood had shifted. Underneath the warmth, a thread of melancholy had woven in.

The General raised a toast. "To Sensai!"

Dozens of cups lifted in reply.

"To Sensai!"

He bowed. "Thank you."

The celebration rolled on. A little quieter, a little more reflective. But still full of community. Gratitude. Love.

Later that evening, as the last of the cookies were packed away and the folding chairs began their slow migration back to garages and porches. A small group walked Sensai back toward The Lodge. The Trophy sat in its new home on a shelf, under a small spotlight someone had rigged up with an extension cord and a lot of duct tape.

The Destroyer looked at it for a long time, arms crossed.

"Y'know," he said finally, "That thing looks pretty good in here."

"Looks even better in our hands," The General said.

Mr. Annoying sighed dramatically. "At least we're retiring undefeated."

Sensai, already halfway to the door, turned.

"You sure about that?" he asked.

And with that, he stepped outside.

A Celebration

———

Every chair was taken. Every table was covered in checkered tablecloths and homemade desserts. The room buzzed with the warm, chaotic energy of a church potluck meets sports banquet if the sport was slow, underhanded, and best played with a cold drink nearby.

Bocce-themed cupcakes formed a pyramid on the dessert table, each topped with a little edible ball made of frosting and colored sugar. There were cookies shaped like measuring sticks. Someone had even crafted a bocce ball out of Rice Krispies and stuck it on a skewer for easy passing.

In the corner, a projector played a slideshow on the wall. Photos faded in and out: Sensai with his foot perfectly placed at the foul line; The General scowling at a measurement; The Destroyer mid-throw, sandwich in one hand, bocce ball in the other. There were pictures from league nights, tournament days, post-game ice cream runs, and more than a few candid shots of Mr. Annoying looking completely unaware he was being photographed.

Every table had a centerpiece featuring a miniature bocce court made from green felt and popsicle sticks.

When Sensai walked through the front doors, the room rose as one.

The applause started soft, the kind people give when a movie ends well. It grew into a standing ovation, with clapping, whistling, and even a few hoots and hollers that made him raise one bushy eyebrow. He didn't wave or bow. He just smiled, deeply and humbly, and nodded in that quiet, mountain-still way of his.

He moved through the crowd like a well-worn stone through a stream. People leaned in to shake his hand, clap his shoulder, or sneak in one last bit of advice.

"Don't forget us."

"Come back next season."

"My backhand's still garbage without you yelling at me."

At the front of the room, under a hand-painted "Farewell, Sensai" sign someone had made in a hurry but with a lot of heart, stood a small wooden podium. Next to it, placed on a low pedestal, was a gift.

A single bocce ball, polished smooth, mounted on a wooden base with a brass plate. The engraving read: "Still Teaching Us."

Sensai stepped forward and stared at it for a long, quiet moment.

The Destroyer elbowed The General. "You think he's gonna cry?"

"Nope," The General said, arms crossed. "But you might."

"I'm might!" The Destroyer whispered.

Once everyone had found their seats and plates of cookies, the speeches began.

First up was Dorina from the Tuesday Morning League, known for her terrifying accuracy and total lack of patience for nonsense. She told the story of how Sensai had once coached her through the yips by making her throw twenty balls in silence, then twenty more with a mariachi album blasting in her earbuds.

"He taught me to calm my mind," she said, eyes a little misty. "Even when my mind is screaming and someone's weed whacking behind Court Two."

The crowd laughed. Sensai smiled but said nothing.

Next was Mark from Facilities, who'd never played bocce in his life but swore Sensai once helped him back up his truck using only hand signals and Zen.

Then came Dave, the league's unofficial social chair, who ran through a list of Sensai's "firsts": first to arrive for games, first to help new players, first to bring ginger tea to potlucks "even though no one knew what to do with it."

And then it was Mr. Annoying's turn.

He walked to the podium, visor askew, gripping a crumpled piece of paper like it was the Gettysburg Address. The room tensed. It was hard to say if people were nervous or preparing to sit through a lot of metaphors.

"Alright," he began, clearing his throat. "So I wrote a thing. And I'm gonna read the thing."

He paused, scanned the room like he was checking wind speed, and began.

"People always say Sensai is calm. They say he's wise. That he's like some kind of bocce wizard from the mountains."

Scattered laughter.

"But what I think he really is... is patient. Patient enough to teach us. To teach me."

He glanced down at the paper, then stuffed it in his pocket.

"I talk too much. We all know that."

"Understatement," someone muttered.

"But Sensai never told me to shut up. He showed me what it looked like to be quiet. And focused. And good at something for the sake of being good at it. Not for applause. Not for trophies."

He nodded toward the mounted bocce ball. "That thing back there? He doesn't need it. We do. So we don't forget."

It was quiet for a beat too long.

Then the applause started again. Lighter this time. A little blurry-eyed.

Mr. Annoying shuffled back to the table, pretending not to wipe his eyes. The Destroyer gave him a firm pat on the back. The General nodded once. High praise from him.

The last speaker of the night was Sensai himself.

He stood. No notes. No jokes. Just his calm presence, amplified by silence.

"I have taught many of you," he said. "But I have also learned. You reminded me that joy and friendship don't retire. That competition can still be fun. That it's okay to care about a game that involves colored balls and measuring tapes."

Laughter again, softer.

"I'm leaving not because I'm tired. I'm leaving because it's time. I am full of gratitude for all you have shared with me. And I am better for having known each of you."

He looked around the room, and for once, his eyes glistened.

"Thank you."

He bowed, just enough to make it feel ancient sacred, and true.

The crowd rose once more.

Toasts were made. Cookies passed hands again. Someone turned the music up a notch. Conversations restarted like engines warming up. Just as someone hit play on a second round of the slideshow and the cupcakes were beginning to dwindle, the double doors to The Lodge opened with a soft creak.

All heads turned.

Standing in the doorway was Lauren, the community lifestyle director, clipboard in one hand and something small and white in the other. She wore her usual "I love my job, but y'all make it hard" smile.

"Sorry to interrupt," she called out over the music. "But I have a little... surprise."

She stepped forward, holding up an envelope. It was official-looking, crisp, cream-colored, and heavy enough to suggest either bad news or very, very good news.

Sensai raised an eyebrow. The General leaned forward. Mr. Annoying whispered, "Is this a bill?"

Lauren cleared her throat and unfolded the paper inside.

"Dear Dell Webb The Woodlands Bocce Team," she began, her voice rising enough to be heard over the soft music. "Congratulations on your recent victory at the Hill Country State Bocce Center Tournament. Your sportsmanship, skill, and community spirit were noted by both officials and fans alike."

A few claps started to rise. Lauren held up a finger.

"It is with great pleasure that the Texas Senior Bocce Association formally invites your team to compete in this year's Texas Senior Bocce Tournament, to be held this fall in College Station."

That's when the clapping erupted, cheers, whistles, and a few wild whoops filled the air. The Destroyer stood up so fast he knocked over a half-full lemonade cup. Mr. Annoying let out a noise that was half laugh, half hiccup. The General smiled.

"We're goin' to Nationals!" someone yelled from the back.

But the excitement lasted only a few seconds.

The room paused. A ripple of hesitation that spread like a hush rolling through dry leaves. The cheers softened. The smiles wavered.

All eyes turned toward Sensai.

He was still standing near the gift table, hands behind his back, that same quiet smile on his face. But he didn't say anything. And he didn't nod.

Because he wouldn't be there.

The realization settled over the room like a soft weight. The Destroyer sat back down, his grin fading. The General shifted in his seat. Mr. Annoying let his raised hands drop into his lap.

Mr. Annoying let his raised hands drop into his lap." We can't do it without him."

A few others murmured in agreement. The DWTW crew looked at one another but didn't speak.

The buzz that had lifted the room a minute earlier had drifted off, replaced by something quieter. A sense of reality returning, like the aftertaste of a too-sweet drink. Winning at Fredericksburg had been lightning in a bottle. A perfect storm of old skill, good timing, and Sensai's steady hand.

Without him, it wouldn't be the same.

Lauren lowered the letter. "I told them I'd pass the message along. No pressure. But... it's kind of a big deal."

No one answered.

Until Sensai stepped forward.

He didn't raise his voice. He didn't need to.

"Why not?" he asked.

The room stayed still.

Sensai looked from face to face, The General, The Destroyer, Mr. Annoying, and then out to the rest of the crowd.

"Do you think I carried that team by myself?" he asked. "You all heard about the games. The shots. The teamwork. Mr. Annoying made the throw of the tournament."

"That was mostly luck," Mr. Annoying muttered.

"No, it wasn't," Sensai said without hesitation.

He turned to The General. "You called every shot with the precision of a chess master."

The General didn't say anything, but his jaw clenched.

"And Destroyer?" Sensai added. "You brought heart. Power. Joy."

The Destroyer stared at the floor like a kid being complimented at graduation.

"You don't need me to play. You never did. I was a reminder."

"Of what?" someone asked.

Sensai smiled. "That we're better than we think we are."

A long pause followed. Not heavy, but thoughtful. Mr. Annoying scratched his chin. The General looked toward their hard-won prize still glowing under the rigged-up spotlight.

Finally, The Destroyer leaned back and let out a breath. "We'd need a fourth."

"Maybe," said Mr. Annoying, glancing around the room. "We hold a round robin. The winner gets the slot."

"That could work," The General said, his voice gravelly but firm. "Keep it in the community."

Sensai nodded. "Let the court decide."

Lauren, still holding the letter, raised her eyebrows. "So... is that a yes?"

Sensai didn't answer. He didn't need to.

The Destroyer cracked his knuckles. "Better dust off the measuring tapes."

Mr. Annoying stood and stretched. "Time to update my highlight reel."

The General, after a moment's silence, simply said: "We're in."

The room erupted again, but this time, the cheers were grounded, not just excitement, but resolve. Laughter returned to the room, followed by a flurry of talk about brackets, schedules, and who was not allowed to serve as judge.

And Sensai?

He stood, hands folded in front of him, that same peaceful look in his eyes.

Final Frame

The Round Robin Tournament began with all the ceremony of a small-town bake sale and the tension of a championship prizefight. The Lodge's front bulletin board became the bracket hub, with names scribbled in marker and match times squeezed between water aerobics flyers and HOA reminders. A lawn chair army formed along the courts each morning, iced coffee in hand, sun visors adjusted like helmets.

At first, it was mostly laughs. "Just for fun," someone said. "Let's see what we've got," said another. As the games rolled on, something shifted. The light-hearted matches turned intense. People started practicing in the evenings. Notes were taken. Tensions rose like the Texas heat.

And then, the surprises began.

Some of the expected favorites, the self-appointed bocce big shots, the ones who always barked tips from the sidelines, cracked under pressure like a fresh batch of peanut brittle. Their throws went wide. Their measurements got shaky. One player accidentally bounced his ball off the wrong rail and then tried to blame the slope.

"I swear that court leans," he muttered.

Others, the quiet ones, the unsure ones, the ones who had never quite believed they belonged, started to shine.

And no one shone brighter than Peggy and Dorina.

Peggy, a retired teacher with a killer aim and a sweet spot for chocolate chip cookies, moved up the ranks. She never talked smack. Never second-guessed. She just stepped up, rolled her throw, and went back to sipping her iced tea.

Dorina was trickier. She played with flair, always trying a little spin, a little trick shot. Sometimes it worked. Sometimes it didn't. But when it did, people took notice. Especially The Destroyer, who started calling her "The Curve" after a shot that looped around three balls and snuck up next to the pallino like it was invited for dinner.

By the last week of the tournament, the bracket was down to four: Peggy, Dorina, and two longtime members of the DWTW Men's League, Dave, and Ned, who were both more shocked than proud to have made it that far.

"Never thought I'd outlast Sarge," said, shaking his head.

"That's because he melted," someone whispered. "Did you see him? Looked like a popsicle with bad form."

Meanwhile, Sensai, who hadn't moved yet, took up a quiet post on the sideline. He coached without coaching. Offered suggestions with the softness of a breeze.

"Shift your stance," he told Dorina one day. "Balance comes from the center."

To Peggy, he only said, "You don't need to think about it. Your throw speaks for you."

They listened. Everyone did.

It was time for the final test.

The last four competitors were invited to face off against the Champs, Sensai, The General, The Destroyer, and Mr. Annoying, in one final match. This was Sensai's last game with the group before his move. Whoever showed the most grit, grace, and game would take his place on the official DWTW team at the state championship.

The crowd showed up early. People brought lawn chairs, sunglasses, and snacks. Someone even dragged a box fan down from The Lodge and plugged it in with a mile of extension cord. A bocce ball-shaped cake sat on a folding table, waiting for post-match celebrations.

The match began under a cloudless sky.

From the first frame, it was clear this wasn't going to be some casual throw-around. Dave opened it with a clean roll that clipped the pallino. Dorina followed with a gutsy power shot that scattered the Champs' blockers. Ned's game tightened under pressure, he stopped overthinking and let the throws fly. Peggy, steady as ever, dropped a point-winner so close to the pallino that even the judges cheered.

The Champs weren't taking it easy either.

The Destroyer threw like a man avenging a bad lunch. The General's strategy was airtight. Mr. Annoying, oddly focused, let his throws speak louder than his commentary. And Sensai played like the breeze. Every roll deliberate. Every move was graceful. Even now, you couldn't tell if he was playing to win or to teach one final lesson.

The lead bounced back and forth. 3–2. Then 5–3. Then 6–7. The crowd got louder. No one sat still.

In the late frames, the score stood at 11–9 in favor of the Champs. Peggy stepped up, eyes sharp. She rolled. Clean. Precise. Perfect. A point.

Then Ned. A power shot. Another point.

11–11.

Sensai took the final throw.

He paused and took a breath. Released.

The ball kissed the edge of the pallino and settled into place like it belonged there all along.

Final score: 12–11.

The Champs had won.

Applause burst across the courts. The four challengers were swarmed with pats on the back, shouted compliments, and a few wide-eyed whispers of "I thought she was just the cookie lady!"

Sensai stood at the center of the court, silent for a moment.

Then he walked toward challengers, smiling.

"You have the calm and you have the fire."

Sensai looked at The General, The Destroyer, and even Mr. Annoying, who was already miming an imaginary trophy lift.

Then, he turned back to Peggy.

"You bring more than your throws," he said. "You bring the whole community with you. Every cookie. Every kind word. Every game you played when no one else wanted to."

He paused.

"If anyone's going to take my spot... it should be you."

The crowd exploded. Peggy's hands flew to her mouth. Someone yelled, "COOKIE MONSTER!" and the name stuck like peanut butter to the roof of the community's heart.

The Destroyer gave her a bear hug. The General nodded in solemn approval. Mr. Annoying offered her his visor, which she wisely declined.

Slices of the bocce ball cake were passed around. A second speaker started blasting Sinatra again. And under the late afternoon sun, the DWTW bocce family celebrated a new chapter.

Sensai stood off to the side for a moment, watching the team laugh, joke, and welcome Cookie Monster into the fold.

He smiled and quietly stepped away from the court, one last time.

He's Still Coaching

Practice began the Monday after the final roster was set.

The courts at DWTW were busier than usual, the pallino was polished and the bocce balls were arranged like a sacred offering. A printed schedule appeared on the community board, four practices a week, plus interleague scrimmages, weather permitting.

The team showed up early, water bottles in hand, and sunblock on ears and elbows. But something was off.

The throws were decent. The pace was there. But the spark felt like it had drifted off with Sensai, carried away on whatever breeze took him to his new zip code.

The Destroyer muttered more. The General got quiet. Mr. Annoying talked even more than usual as if trying to fill a silence none of them could name. And Cookie Monster, bless her, kept showing up with peanut butter chocolate chip fuel, like it would fix everything.

Some days, they were fire. Crisp rolls. Tight groupings. Calm strategy. Other days, they looked like four people who'd met at a bus stop and decided to try a new hobby. They lost a practice game to a team from the next retirement community over. It stung more than they let on.

"You know what Sensai would say?" Cookie Monster offered after one particularly rough match.

The Destroyer sighed. "That we played with too much tension in our knees and too little in our heads."

"No," she smiled. "He'd say, 'Shake it off. Then stretch. In that order.'"

The General cracked a rare grin. "He did say that."

Mr. Annoying pointed a finger in the air. "And then he'd drink his weird tea and beat us with grace."

The tension loosened a bit. The silence began to break. The team found its rhythm again, not by replacing Sensai, but by remembering how he made them better, together.

The tournament arrived like a Texas storm, loud, fast-moving, and hard to ignore.

The parking lot at the State Senior Bocce Tournament was full before 9 a.m. Someone from DWTW had chartered a shuttle bus. Someone else made signs. One woman painted her face with a tiny white pallino on each cheek and wore a shirt that said "Sensai Sent Me."

The stands were full. The breeze carried the smell of popcorn, sunscreen, and anticipation. On the south court, under the banner that read National Senior Bocce Tournament – State Finals, the DWTW team took their places.

This wasn't like last year.

Last year they wore mismatched hats and shirts that had seen better decades. This year, they wore fresh, pressed team shirts, deep forest green with bold white lettering: DWTW BOCCE. On the sleeve, a small patch: a hand-drawn crown sitting atop a bocce ball.

On the sidelines, a handful of cheerleaders in matching visors and pom-poms chanted:

> Don't worry, throw well! Play hard, play swell!
>
> D! W! T! W! Bocce strong, we excel!"

Mr. Annoying wept openly at the cheer. Claimed it was allergies. No one believed him.

The first few matches flew by. The DWTW team played smart. Clean. Calm. They didn't dominate, but they didn't crumble. Cookie Monster nailed two precision shots that spun so perfectly they were accused of witchcraft. The

Destroyer rediscovered his fire. The General orchestrated every strategy like a battlefield map. And Mr. Annoying... well, he talked too much, but his throws backed it up.

They moved through the bracket like a slow-rolling storm.

By the final day, they were one of two teams left standing.

The championship match was scheduled for the afternoon. The sun was relentless. The crowd was louder than ever. Someone held up a sign that read, "COOKIE MONSTER FOR PRESIDENT."

Their opponents were no joke, a team from El Paso known for precision, silence, and playing in matching long-sleeved shirts like they didn't believe in sweat. They were good. Real good.

The match was tight.

Points were swapped like poker chips. No one got more than a two-point lead. Every frame had the crowd holding their breath. The General landed a clutch roll that kissed the pallino so softly it drew gasps. Mr. Annoying celebrated with a backflip that was more of a lean-and-hope.

With the score at 11–11, the final frame began.

The Destroyer opened strong. The General followed with a clean block. But the El Paso team was unshaken. They danced their throws between the DWTW defense like they'd drawn a map to the pallino.

Cookie Monster's final throw was beautiful, straight, soft, sure. It nestled near the pallino like a faithful pet.

One final roll.

It curved, dipped, and tapped Cookie Monster's ball then stopped half an inch closer.

Final score: 12–11. El Paso

Second place.

There was a moment of silence. Not disappointment. Just the breath you take when you come so close, you can almost taste it.

The medals were silver, but they sparkled like gold under the afternoon sun. The announcer handed them out with fanfare. Photos were taken. Cheers rang out.

But still, Sensai lingered in their thoughts.

They hadn't brought the trophy home.

They hadn't won it for him.

As if on cue, The General pulled a folded note from her pocket.

"He mailed this last week," he said quietly. "Said not to open it until the end."

He unfolded the letter and read it aloud.

To my team—my friends.

Winning is a beautiful thing. But growth? That's everything.

You've played with honor. You've played with heart. And if you're reading this, you've made it to the end.

Remember this: The mark of a great player isn't in how they throw, but in how they lift their team.

I am proud of you.

Always.

Now go celebrate. And someone brings me a cookie.

— Sensai

No one spoke for a long time.

The General gave a small, tight smile. "He's still coaching," he said.

And just like that, the sadness cracked open into joy. They celebrated. They posed with their medals. The DWTW cheerleaders broke into a freestyle chant.

Second place had never felt more like a win.

As the sun began its slow dip behind the trees, the DWTW bocce team stood together, shirts pressed, medals shining, hearts full, knowing that greatness isn't about the trophy.

It's about the journey. The cookies. The community. And the friends who help you throw well, even when they're not beside you.

The Menace

No one remembers exactly when "The Menace" appeared at the DWTW courts. One day, he wasn't there. The next, he was. Another new face watching from the sidelines, arms crossed, hat pulled low, eyes tracking every roll like a hawk.

He didn't say much at first. He offered polite nods and the occasional "Nice shot." When someone invited him to play because, at DWTW, you never sat long before someone tossed you a ball. He stepped up and rolled one of the smoothest throws anyone had seen from a so-called "new guy."

"Beginner's luck," someone muttered. But after the third or fourth pinpoint throw, even The General gave a little grunt of acknowledgment.

It wasn't long before he found himself under Sensai's quiet mentorship. It was not a formal thing. Sensai didn't do formal. It was more a matter of proximity. They'd finish games and end up standing near each other watching. When Sensai offered a, "You rush your follow-through," or "Your balance is in your heels," The Menace nodded and absorbed it like the sun on a stone.

No one ever called him "The Menace" to his face. Not at first.

The name was born in whispers. At first, a bit of a joke. Someone said, "That new guy's a menace with that final throw," after he flipped a losing round into a walk-off win for the third time in a week. The nickname stuck like a burr.

Soon, everyone was using it, with affection, awe, and a hint of fear. He was a menace in the best possible way. Calm under pressure. Lethal when the game was on the line. He didn't trash talk much. He would line up his shot, take a breath, and let the ball do the talking.

He became the go-to anchor. Players shuffled teams to have him go last. If there was a match where someone had to clean up the chaos and turn hope into points, they'd look over and say, "We got The Menace, we're fine."

Even the legends—The General, Cookie Monster, The Destroyer—started taking notes. Someone swore they saw The General with a small spiral notebook after a game.

The Return of Sensai

The courts at DWTW had always been lively, but in the months following the senior tournament, something shifted. Bocce went from a retirement hobby to a way of life. It started with a casual shift from three days a week to five. Then someone said, "Why not Saturdays?" Then, "Well, we're already here Sunday for coffee, might as well roll a few." Before long, it was seven days of bocce, rain permitting and sometimes not even then.

A women-only league was formed, and they were no joke. They practiced twice as hard and talked twice as little. They showed up with matching visors and left with matching wins. Someone tried to call them "The Glitter Gang," but after getting beaten three times in a row, they stopped.

The quality of play across the community went up. New blood came in. Trick shots became standard. Strategies evolved. Even Mr. Annoying toned down his commentary in favor of studying his rivals. You couldn't get away with lazy rolls anymore. Every game was a lesson. Every mistake was noticed.

Through it all, The Menace kept getting better. Sharper angles. More finesse. Always the last one to throw, always the one who mattered most when it counted.

Sensai had always been the quiet center of the court. After he left, his presence stuck around like the smell of cedar after rain. Subtle, grounding, hard to describe but easy to feel.

At first, folks kept in touch. Sensai sent emails, the occasional postcard, and a photo of his new courts in Hot Springs, flat, with a view of pine trees. He wrote updates about the team he was playing with. He mentioned his son-in-law, "The Mathematician," who could measure by eye with scary precision. He always closed with something humble. "Keep rolling. I miss y'all."

As time passed, so did the frequency of updates. Life got full. Games picked up. Sensai became more memory than presence.

Still, he was everywhere.

When someone landed a tricky shot, someone else would say, "That's one for Sensai." If a player flubbed a roll and looked embarrassed, someone would murmur, "Balance from the center," and it would be okay again.

Players joked about who might be the next Sensai, but it was always a joke. The title wasn't up for grabs. Sensai had earned it the way only time, grace, and patience can. No one dared say, "I'm the new Sensai," because everyone knew it didn't work that way.

The fall air rolled in with the kind of quiet confidence that Sensai himself used to bring to the court. The leaves were beginning to change, with a little rust at the edges, and a little gold creeping into the green. It was the kind of day where the breeze carried the sound of a good bocce shot farther than usual.

Most folks at DWTW were scattered, some in lawn chairs or the pool, some organizing for the next event, and others lingering by the snack table debating whether the cookies were store-bought or homemade. It was Cookie Monster who saw him first.

"Is that—" she whispered, setting down a plate of peanut butter chocolate chips.

The General looked up. The Destroyer nearly dropped his measuring tape.

Sensai stood beyond the court's fence line, hands folded in front of him, a small duffel over one shoulder, the same straw hat perched atop his head like time hadn't passed. He smiled, calm, effortless, and a touch mischievous.

"Now there's a ghost from the golden age," muttered Mr. Annoying.

The scrape of chairs shouted greetings and scuffing shoes echoed across the court like the opening beat of a celebration. They moved toward him in a wave, players who had trained under him, competed beside him, and still told stories about that one angle bank shot he made back in '22.

"I thought you moved to Hot Springs and became a legend in exile," said Cookie Monster as she gave him a careful hug.

"I am not a legend," Sensai replied, "I am just a man with bad knees and patient children."

"Well, you look exactly the same," said The General, offering his hand.

"I've aged five bocce seasons," Sensai said. "That's like dog years."

Laughter bloomed.

They played a few friendly rounds that afternoon, more reunion than competition. The court felt different with Sensai there. His throws were still elegant like the ball always wanted to land where he willed it. And his advice? Always vague and always, exactly what you needed.

"Eyes forward, but throw with memory," he told Peggy.

"What does that even mean?" she muttered before she nailed a perfect throw.

The Menace had been at DWTW for almost a year before Sensai left. Most people hadn't paid much attention to him at first. Sensai had. He was the first to nod after a particularly clean roll and offer a short, approving, "Good control."

From that moment on, The Menace made sure he was paying attention, not only to the game but to how Sensai moved, and how he taught without teaching. That year under Sensai's quiet watch had stuck with him.

Now, seeing Sensai again older, but still precise brought a strange kind of calm. He wasn't nervous. He was ready.

The group had finished a third friendly match when Sensai turned to The Menace, who had thrown the final point.

"Good shot," Sensai said. "Reminds me of a throw I saw once."

The Menace blinked. "You mean one of yours?"

Sensai smiled. "No, it was yours. About one minute ago."

That earned a round of laughter. Even The General cracked a smile, which, by his standards, was a full-blown belly laugh.

Later, after the sun had dipped low and someone lit the bug-repellent torches, a small circle formed around the picnic tables. Old stories made their rounds, like when Mr. Annoying measured a ball with a shoe and argued he was right. Or the time Cookie Monster won a match with a "snack break strategy" that distracted the other team mid-frame.

Sensai sipped from a thermos. "This tea is better when it's shared," he said, passing it around.

The Challenge

⸻

It was so casual it almost slipped past them.

"You know," Sensai said, brushing dust off a bocce bag," if you youngins ever want to come play against a real team..." He let the sentence hang in the air like an unclaimed prize.

Mr. Annoying immediately perked up. "Was that a challenge?"

"No, no," Sensai said, holding up a hand. "More of an open invitation. Our courts in Hot Springs are nice. Real level. Great shade. We've got a Tuesday group that plays like it's the finals every match."

The General raised an eyebrow. "You putting together a retirement dream team over there?"

"Well," Sensai said, "my son-in-law plays now. We call him 'The Mathematician.' He calculates throws with geometry-level precision and carries a small notepad during games. It's... unsettling."

"I don't like that," muttered Cookie Monster. "Sounds like he'd argue with a ruler."

"He only argues with the laws of physics," said Sensai. "And sometimes he wins."

The Menace was already picturing it, new courts, new faces, the smell of pine trees, and possibility. He glanced at his own teammates. They weren't what they used to be, they were better. Stronger. Smarter. More bonded than ever.

"Well," The Menace said with a shrug, "we could come up... just to make sure your legend holds up."

Sensai gave him a long, amused look. "You want to test the teacher?"

"No," The Menace said, meeting his eyes. "I'm curious how the teacher handles being the underdog."

The court went quiet for a beat, then roared with laughter, clapping backs, and half-shouts of "oooh!" and "he went there!"

Sensai bowed his head. "Fair enough."

By the end of the night, it was no longer a joke. The idea had taken root, like a fresh chalk line on a blank court.

They started discussing logistics. Who could make the trip. Who'd stay behind. The Destroyer had knee rehab. The General had family visiting. So The Menace would anchor. Cookie Monster was a given. Mr. Annoying claimed he was already packed. And after some debate, The Drifter was nominated, partly for his high-risk throws, partly for his eternal optimism, and partly for his commentary that rivaled Mr. Annoying.

Before they left, Sensai smiled at them from the court's edge. "Remember," he said. "It's not about proving something."

"What's it about then?" asked Cookie Monster.

Sensai looked out at the shadows stretching across the court. "Respect. Joy. And a good measuring tape."

The morning after Sensai's visit, a paper sign appeared on the DWTW bulletin board next to the HOA meeting reminder and a lost cat notice that had been there since April. It was scrawled in Mr. Annoying's handwriting:

BOCCE GOES ON TOUR

HOT SPRINGS OR BUST

Below it, four names: The Menace. The Drifter. Cookie Monster. Mr. Annoying. Someone had drawn a crown over The Menace's name and someone else had crossed it out and replaced it with a very tiny mustache.

Absent were The General and The Destroyer, who had both offered their regrets with solemn head nods and vague references to "prior obligations," which turned out to be a granddaughter's recital and a cortisone injection.

The Menace, already the anchor of most casual games, accepted the role without flair or fuss. He wasn't loud about his confidence. He didn't need to be. His game spoke for itself, quiet hands, sharp eyes, and a throw so consistent it made the measuring tape unnecessary.

The Drifter, who had earned his name from his unpredictable throws, was the spark plug of the group. He showed up with more energy than a bag of coffee beans and was known to yell things like "Ride the rail, baby!" or "OK, Throw all your bullets." He brought chaos, but also magic.

Cookie Monster remained the group's heartbeat. She still baked before matches. Still kept a close eye on the courts and made sure no one forgot their water bottles. Anyone who mistook her kindness for softness hadn't seen her drop a roll two millimeters from the pallino three frames in a row.

Mr. Annoying... was still Mr. Annoying. His commentary hadn't slowed down. The excitement of an away match only seemed to fuel him. He was already drafting "travel chants" and suggesting custom warm-up routines no one asked for. Underneath all the chatter, the man could throw.

"New team," The Menace said one afternoon, watching them run drills. "Same fire."

Cookie Monster handed him a cookie. "Just try not to burn anything down."

Hot Springs or Bust

They left at 6:42 a.m. on a Thursday, delayed only when Mr. Annoying insisted on checking if the back tires looked "fully awake."

Cookie Monster rode shotgun with a container of pecan shortbread balanced on her lap like a sacred artifact. The Drifter called dibs on DJ duties and immediately regretted it when the auxiliary cable shorted and left them listening to the same smooth jazz CD Sensai had gifted the community two years ago.

"Not bad," The Menace muttered. "Reminds me of the tempo he played at."

"Yeah," The Drifter said. "Like his bocce balls took naps on the way to the pallino."

Mr. Annoying, driving, let out a laugh. "Hey, remember when he taught that one guy to breathe before every shot and he passed out from exhaling too hard?"

"He said, 'Find your breath,'" Cookie Monster said. "Not 'expel it like a geyser.'"

As the miles rolled by, the mood lightened. The Drifter pointed out every suspiciously-shaped cloud. Mr. Annoying kept guessing what Sensai's new team might be like.

"I bet they wear polos," he said. "Matching polos."

"I bet the Mathematician keeps score with Roman numerals," said The Drifter.

"I bet Sensai's team does pregame tai chi," Mr. Annoying said.

Cookie Monster chuckled. "I bet they show up and play like he taught us."

The Menace hadn't said much. He sat behind the driver, gazing out the window. Occasionally, his lips moved like he was reciting something to himself.

"You nervous?" Cookie Monster asked, passing back a shortbread.

He shook his head. "No. Just... remembering."

She smiled. "That's how you know you're ready."

The Drifter turned down the music. "You think he meant it? That 'real team' thing?"

"Oh, he meant it," The Menace said. "But not the way you think."

"What do you mean?"

"He didn't say 'better team.' He said 'real team.' That means one that plays like it matters. Win or lose."

Mr. Annoying nodded. "You think he's setting us up?"

"No," Cookie Monster said. "I think he's pushing us to play like we mean it."

They all sat with that for a while, letting the idea settle in with the hum of the tires.

By early afternoon, the landscape had shifted, with more trees, older brick buildings, and that faint whiff of mineral water that marked the edges of Hot Springs proper. They pulled into the small lot beside the community center where the courts were located.

Pulling up to the Hot Springs bocce facility was like stepping into a postcard of small-town charm. The courts were nestled beside a winding river that caught the late afternoon sun, shimmering gold and blue. Meticulously groomed grass framed the smooth clay courts, and rows of benches waited patiently for spectators. Flags fluttered overhead, their colors bright against the sky. A hand-painted sign read:

Welcome DWTW — Let's Roll.

The Menace, Cookie Monster, The Drifter, and Mr. Annoying piled out of the car, stretching limbs cramped from the long drive. The scent of fresh-cut grass mingled with a faint hint of eucalyptus from nearby trees. The world felt different here, slower, quieter, but ready for something big.

"Polos," muttered Mr. Annoying. "I told you."

Sensai was already there, leaning against the fence, his trademark smile lighting up his weathered face. His eyes crinkled the way they always did when he saw a friend. Beside him stood the Mathematician, younger, sharp as a tack, tape measure in hand, adjusting his stance with geometric precision. He didn't wave, he nodded.

"He looks like he measures his coffee grounds with a ruler," said The Drifter.

"Welcome to the court, gentlemen," Sensai said, his voice low but full of warmth. "I see the rumors weren't exaggerated. You actually came."

Mr. Annoying grinned. "You said we should visit.' We took that as a dare."

The Menace grinned. "We came to see what a real team looks like."

Sensai raised an eyebrow. "Hope you brought sunglasses."

Cookie Monster stepped forward with a basket of cookies she'd baked that morning, pecan shortbread, the group's favorite. Sensai took two and offered the other to the Mathematician.

The Mathematician accepted it, nodding with mock seriousness. "This is the best opening move I've seen all season."

Over the next two days, the courts buzzed with activity. Matches unfolded under the bright sky, with the warm sun casting long shadows and the occasional cool breeze providing relief.

They didn't bother with formal teams the first day. No rosters or matchups, only laughter, loose lineups, and players drifting onto the court with balls in hand and smiles ready. The moment enough players were present, the games began.

The Menace found himself paired with a lanky Hot Springs player known as The Whisper, famous for throwing so softly you could barely hear the ball land. Cookie Monster ended up alongside Slick, a veteran with a slicked-back ponytail and a knack for sliding his ball right between opponents' defenses.

"Name's Slick," he said, tossing a warm-up shot that stopped dead beside the pallino.

"You live up to it?" Cookie Monster asked, arms crossed.

"I flirt with it," he grinned. "But I never cheat."

She handed him a pecan shortbread cookie. "Then we're gonna get along fine."

Mr. Annoying was everywhere at once. He moved from team to team between games, claiming he was scouting. He just wanted to be wherever the most talking was happening. Midway through one match, he grabbed a ball, spun it on his finger like a basketball, and announced, "Ladies and gentlemen, I give you — The Spiral of Destiny."

He launched it with a flourish.

It pinged off one ball, then another, and kissed the pallino before it skidded off to the side rail.

There was a beat of silence.

"That was... something," muttered a Hot Springs player, choking back a laugh.

"Yeah, yeah," Mr. Annoying said. "Wind caught it. I forgot to factor in the humidity. Rookie mistake."

The Drifter, meanwhile, was having a blast, shouting his trademark chants, "Drift, drift, drift!", every time he sent a bocce ball sliding wide. His enthusiasm was infectious, and even the most reserved Hot Springs players found themselves cracking grins and offering high-fives.

"Let it ride!" he whooped after an unintentional bank shot landed in scoring position. "That's the Drift special!"

In a quieter corner of the court, The Menace teamed up with The Mathematician. Their eyes tracked each throw and every subtle angle, both tuned in like detectives watching a mystery unfold. The Menace adjusted his release with a calm confidence that came from countless hours of practice, while The Mathematician studied the court with quiet focus, nodding after each shot as if confirming a winning throw. The grin they shared after a perfect frame said it all. This wasn't about winning; it was about loving the game and having fun doing it.

Between frames, The Menace murmured to Cookie Monster, "It's like chess with spheres."

She smiled. "More like physics and luck." She tossed him a cookie. "You're the luck part."

Sensai strolled the perimeter like a host at a backyard reunion, relaxed and warm. He offered nods and smiles, and the occasional quiet suggestion slipped between throws.

"Try anchoring your heel when you aim," he told a Hot Springs player, clapping him on the back.

He stopped beside The Drifter and raised an eyebrow. "You ever considered aiming before yelling?"

"I yell to aim," The Drifter replied. "Works every third throw."

Then he attempted a no-look backward toss that somehow landed in bounds, causing a burst of applause from both teams. He bowed theatrically and shouted, "Told you!"

Cookie Monster's pecan shortbread became the unofficial currency of the court. She handed one to a wiry player named Daryl after he nailed a delicate sidearm curve around two blockers.

"If that's how y'all power up," he said, wide-eyed, "I'm gonna need that recipe before the weekend's over."

"Secret weapon," she said with a wink.

No one knew what the score was. After three or four games, the teams had blended so many times no one could say for sure who was on which side. What they did know was who threw well under pressure, who liked long-range bombs, who had the softest touch, and who cracked under too much banter.

Mr. Annoying stood near the sidelines narrating between bites of a cookie. "You see that? That's a fade shot. That's what you do when you want your opponent to think they've won."

The Drifter chimed in. "Nah, that's a fluke. We call that a drift drop. Classic misdirection."

"Remember when Sensai told me to 'listen to the court'?" Mr. Annoying said, gesturing wildly.

"Yeah," said The Drifter. "I tried that once. Ended up talking to a squirrel instead."

Cookie Monster didn't even look up. "It told him to drift."

They all cracked up.

By late afternoon, the sun hung low, casting golden light across the smooth sand. Players stood chatting, swapping throw techniques, demonstrating grips, and casually ribbing each other. Someone tried to tally games, but no one cared. The real scoreboard was written in laughs, fist-bumps, and quiet glances that said: you're good.

The menace stood to the side, watching. He saw how Sensai stepped back to let others shine. He felt the game living and breathing, not as competition, but as a community. This was bocce at its best.

The Competition

———

The tournament was laid out clearly from the start: seven games spread over two days. The first team to reach four victories would claim the challenge cup, a modest wooden trophy, carved with the logos of both clubs, symbolic but cherished by everyone involved.

Though the competition was friendly, a serious intensity hung in the air like the crisp morning breeze. Both teams knew the value of the games wasn't in winning, but in honoring the traditions of bocce and the community it fostered.

Each throw was met with respectful silence or cheers, with handshakes and "good shots" called out whether for teammates or opponents. It was like a friendly war fought with smiles, strategy, and sportsmanship.

The opening game set the tone. Cookie Monster's usual calm was on full display. Each throw was meticulous and each ball landed exactly where she intended. Her quiet focus kept the team steady.

The Drifter's approach was a wild contrast. As he stepped onto the court, he shouted, "Let's shake the earth!" before launching a throw that knocked out the Hot Springs blockers.

"Drift, drift, drift!" he called out, pumping his fist as the ball slipped between two opponents, nudging DWTW closer to victory.

As the final ball settled, the score shifted in DWTW's favor, drawing cheers that lifted their spirits and set a hopeful tone for the day.

The Mathematician was a man of precision. Midway through the second game, he lined up a shot that seemed impossible to anyone else.

"Watch the angle," he muttered, taking careful aim.

The bocce ball rolled true, gliding past blockers and landing inches from the pallino.

"That's science, not luck," Mr. Annoying muttered, shaking his head in disbelief.

Hot Springs seized the moment, adding points until they edged out a narrow, hard-fought win.

Sensai's presence was a reminder that legends never fade. He moved with effortless grace, analyzing the court like a master.

Late in the third game, he made a blocking throw so perfect it silenced the crowd.

The ball landed in the path of the Menace's last attempt, enough to disrupt his shot without displacing the pallino.

The Hot Springs crowd erupted in cheers, and even the DWTW team applauded the brilliance of the play.

Facing pressure to keep the tournament balanced, DWTW turned to the Menace.

The score was tied as he stepped forward, the crowd hushed in anticipation.

With a slow, measured throw, he threaded the needle between two Hot Springs balls, gently nudging the pallino.

That impossible shot seemed to defy the odds and sealed the game.

The team erupted in celebration, but the Menace simply nodded.

Exhausted but exhilarated, both teams gathered off the courts as the sun dipped low. The score was tied 2–2, balanced and full of promise.

Laughter mixed with strategic debates about what Day 2 might bring.

"Tomorrow's the real test," Sensai said, clapping The Menace on the back.

The Menace smiled. "We're ready."

The sun rose softer on the second day, its warm fingers slipping across the dew-dusted courts in Hot Springs. A few players arrived early to stretch or sip coffee in quiet clusters. The banter of the day before had settled into a more focused energy.

By midmorning, the bleachers filled again with locals and a growing crowd of curious onlookers who'd heard about the friendly but fierce contest. A pair of retirees sold donuts out of a golf cart marked "Hot Springs Hospitality." One man had even painted a sign: "Respect the Drift" — a reference The Drifter proudly posed in front of.

The score stood at two games apiece. Three matches remained. First team to four wins. No do-overs. No flukes. Just bocce.

DWTW came out humming like a well-tuned machine. It wasn't flashy. It was efficient. Each player did what they needed to do and nothing more.

Cookie Monster placed her shots with surgical grace, lining up near-perfect defenders early in the frame. Mr. Annoying, more focused than usual, called out strategy between unsolicited stories about the time he almost went pro in ping-pong.

Then came The Drifter's moment.

The game was tight, tied at 9–9. Hot Springs had placed two blockers in a tight line, daring someone to punch through.

"I'm feelin' squirrelly," The Drifter said with a grin.

Mr. Annoying threw him a skeptical look. "Please don't say things like that before you throw."

The Drifter lined up, twirled the ball once, and whispered, "Drift... drift... drift..."

The ball slammed the front blocker, spun sideways, clipped the second, and miraculously nudged the pallino their way.

The crowd gasped. The scoreboard flipped. 11–9.

Moments later, DWTW clinched the final point, ending the game 12–9.

If Game 5 was about flair, Game 6 was a master class in discipline.

The Mathematician and Sensai moved like they shared the same mind. Every throw from the younger man was a setup. Every response from Sensai was a finishing touch.

It wasn't how good they were. It was how seamlessly they worked together, like a father-son piano duet where you can't tell who's leading and following.

Mr. Annoying tried to counter with chatter.

"You know what Einstein said about angles?" he quipped, watching The Mathematician measure with string and instinct. "Nothing! He was too busy inventing relativity!"

The Mathematician smiled. Then dropped a shot half an inch from the pallino.

DWTW played well, but it wasn't enough. They missed one block. A soft roll drifted too far. Momentum slipped.

Final score: 12–7, Hot Springs.

Still, the DWTW bench clapped loudly at the buzzer.

"Remind me not to challenge science next time," Mr. Annoying muttered.

The courts quieted.

It wasn't an official championship. There was no trophy table, no announcer with a mic. But you wouldn't have known it by the tension in the air.

Every lawn chair was filled. Every coffee was abandoned. Someone had even silenced the portable speaker playing golden oldies. All eyes were on the court.

The final game began with a near-silent coin flip. DWTW would throw first.

What followed was a masterclass in competition. Both teams played clean, tight, and precise. Nobody blinked. Nobody cracked. Each point was earned.

Back and forth the score climbed.

6–5. 7–7. 9–9. 10–10.

Not a soul moved from their seat. Phones stayed pocketed. This was old-school drama in real-time.

In the second-to-last frame, Hot Springs pulled ahead by one. DWTW answered. Then came the final frame.

11–11.

Cookie Monster placed a beautiful opening ball. The Mathematician answered with a bank shot that kissed it aside and took position. The Drifter threw a bouncer that rattled the defenders but failed to shift the score.

Then came Sensai.

Quiet. Focused. As graceful as he'd ever been.

He took his stance. A soft breath in. A slow exhale. He threw.

The ball curved with elegance, weaved through blockers like it had a homing beacon, and nestled against the pallino with poetic precision.

For a second, nobody made a sound.

Then, an eruption, cheers from the Hot Springs crowd, applause from both benches and even a few gasps from DWTW fans who had seen that shot before.

Sensai stood there, modest, the faintest smile in his eyes.

One throw left.

The Menace stepped forward.

He didn't fidget. He didn't speak. He rolled his shoulders back and stared down the court.

Sensai met him halfway.

"You can do this," he said, not as an opponent, but as a mentor passing the torch.

The Menace gave a small, wry smile. "I know," he said. "My Sensai showed me this."

He crouched low, took a steadying breath, and released the ball.

It moved like it had memory. It traced the same curve Sensai had taken, glided past the same defenders, kissed Sensai's ball enough to shift it a few inches, and took its place beside the pallino.

The court exploded with cheers. Hot Springs players leaped to their feet. DWTW fans shouted themselves hoarse. Even Sensai laughed and clapped, eyes shining as he walked over and pulled The Menace into a hug.

Final score: 12–11. DWTW.

The challenge had been answered.

Passing the Torch

The morning air in Hot Springs was crisp, a touch of fall finally edging out the heavy summer heat. The kind of morning where you almost needed a sweater, but not quite. The DWTW team was in the middle of an unspoken ritual. Suitcases were being shuffled. Coffee was being sipped. Mr. Annoying was already asking where they should stop for lunch on the drive back.

The car was halfway packed when Sensai appeared, walking across the lot with a calm step and a paper tray of steaming breakfast tacos in one hand.

"I figured y'all were about to make the cardinal sin of leaving town without eating," he said, smiling.

"Breakfast and life advice. We're back on brand," Cookie Monster said, accepting the tray like a sacred offering.

"You know," The Drifter said, peering into the bag, "this might be the most emotional moment of my week."

"Second only to you missing that easy roll yesterday," Mr. Annoying jabbed.

"Low blow. But fair."

Sensai chuckled, then turned to look at each of them. His gaze wasn't measuring or instructive like it once was, it was proud. Settled. Warm.

"You have something beautiful, back there at DWTW," he said. "And you four are carrying it forward."

"We had a pretty solid teacher," The Menace offered.

"You still do," Sensai replied, gesturing toward the rest of the team. "Each other."

There was a pause as the moment lingered long enough to feel like something more than a goodbye.

Sensai looked at The Menace.

"You've got a new Sensai now."

There it was. Not a handoff. Not a title. A truth, delivered like all his truths, plainspoken and certain.

The Drifter let out a dramatic gasp. "OH, it's official now. New Sensai. I'm ordering the T-shirts."

Cookie Monster grinned, half-expecting The Menace to roll his eyes, but he didn't. He shook his head with a quiet smile.

"I'm flattered," he said. "But there can only be one. And he's staying here."

Sensai didn't say anything. He just nodded, like someone who knew exactly what was being said between the words.

They hugged. One by one. Sensai stood in the morning sun as they climbed into the car and pulled out of the lot. He raised a hand in farewell.

The Menace, sitting in the back seat, didn't look back. He wasn't thinking about the games anymore. He felt that something had shifted. Sensai hadn't given him a title. He gave him a path to follow.

Back at Del Webb, life moved at its regular, meandering pace.

The courts had seen a little wear in the week they were gone, leaves scattered across the lanes and a dog-walker shoe print right through one of the baselines, but it felt like home.

Inside the main room of The Lodge, the little trophy shelf had gained a new addition.

The Hot Springs Cup now sat beside the polished Second Place medal from the Senior League Finals, and the marvel from Fredericksburg that Mr. Annoying had once tried to use as a paperweight.

Three trophies. Three chapters. Three reminders of what a community could build when the rules were simple: Don't Worry Throw Well, laugh often, and show up.

Later that afternoon, the players gathered on the court. Lawn chairs were lined up. A folding table held a box of cookies with a sticky note: "Courtesy of Cookie Monster. Do not touch until after frame 3." (They were touched immediately.)

The game started as it always did, light banter, half-stretched arms, and someone arguing over who should hold the tape measure.

The Drifter spun a ball in his hand and squinted at the sun. "Perfect day to drift," he said with unwarranted confidence.

"I swear if you say 'drift' one more time, I'm gonna call HOA," Cookie Monster warned.

Laughter rolled across the court.

Midway through the match, one of the newer players, still getting the hang of judging distance lined up a throw. The pallino was stuck in a tough spot, boxed in by a lucky bounce. Not an easy shot.

He squinted, stepped up, rolled the ball between his hands, then murmured, "Let's see if I can Menace this one."

Cookie Monster, standing off to the side, let out a short, delighted laugh. "That's gonna catch on."

The player missed the shot by about three feet. No one cared. They clapped anyway. It wasn't about the throw. It was about the intention. The spirit behind it.

As the sun began to dip low, turning the court gold wed long-shadowed, another game started.

No medals. No speeches. Just friends, rolling forward.

Like Sensai showed them.

A Special thanks to all of the Dell Webb The Woodlands Bocce Players

Al Jack Bill Jim Chuck John

Dave M. Ken Dave P. Matt Don Mike

Dorina Ned Dwayne Nick Ed Peggy

Gary Steve F. Gregg Steve G.

and all the other players who join us on the court.

Don't Worry Throw Well

Don't miss out!

Visit the website below and you can sign up to receive emails whenever Matthew Dean publishes a new book. There's no charge and no obligation.

https://books2read.com/r/B-A-VRFXD-MRGOG

BOOKS 2 READ

Connecting independent readers to independent writers.

Also by Matthew Dean

Driven
Don't Worry Throw Well

About the Author

Matthew Dean is a writer whose work explores the intersections of memory, identity, and the human experience. Inspired by both personal journeys and universal truths, his stories invite readers into narratives rich with depth and authenticity. He lives in Houston, Texas, where he continues to write and reflect on the paths that shape us.